We Are No More

By Bryce Courtney

BOOK ONE:

Story of Loss

Jonas stared out at the desolate ruins of the city, the once bustling streets now littered with debris and the remnants of destroyed buildings. The eerie silence was only broken by the distant sounds of screeching monsters that roamed the empty streets, their horrifying presence sending shivers down his spine.

He had been trapped in this nightmare for what felt like an eternity, the monsters lurking around every corner, their twisted forms haunting his every step. The memory of the day the creatures first appeared was etched into his mind - the chaos, the screams, the desperate fight for survival as people were mercilessly slaughtered before his eyes.

But somehow, against all odds, Jonas had managed to survive. Along with a small group of fellow survivors, they had banded together, finding shelter in the remains of a once grand hotel. They lived in constant fear, always on the lookout for the next attack, never knowing if they would see another day.

As days turned into weeks, hope began to fade. The monsters seemed to grow stronger, their numbers increasing with each passing day. Food and supplies were running low, and the survivors knew that their time was running out.

Jonas stood at the edge of the cliff, his heart heavy with the weight of his choices. The sun dipped below the horizon, casting a golden hue over the turbulent sea below. Memories flooded his mind, memories of laughter, love, and loss.

He remembered Sarah's smile, how her laughter had once filled their tiny sanctuary with warmth amidst the darkness. She had been his anchor, his reason to keep fighting when all seemed lost. But now, she was gone, taken by the merciless creatures that prowled the night.

As Jonas gazed out over the restless ocean, a bitter wind whipped at his tattered clothes. His fingers traced the edge of a crumpled photograph he kept tucked into his pocket - a snapshot of happier times when the world was still whole and filled with promise. Now, that world lay in ruins, a mere echo of its former self.

A distant howl echoed through the twilight, snapping Jonas back to the present. He knew they were closing in, drawn by the scent of dwindling hope that clung to him like a cloak. His fellow survivors had huddled inside, seeking solace in fading memories and whispered prayers. But Jonas couldn't bring himself to join them, not tonight.

With a heavy heart, he stepped closer to the edge, peering down into the churning depths below. The sea beckoned to him, its waves crashing against jagged rocks with a hypnotic rhythm. He imagined plunging into its embrace, letting go of the pain and fear that had become his constant companions.

A sudden movement caught his eye from the corner of the cliff. Sarah's voice, soft and lilting, whispered in his mind, urging him to remember their dreams, their plans for a future beyond this nightmare. Tears welled up in his eyes as he clutched the photograph tightly to his chest, a last reminder of the love they had shared.

But as the shadows lengthened and the creatures drew nearer, Jonas knew that his time had run out. With a final, anguished cry that was lost in the wind, he let himself fall forward, surrendering to the abyss below.

The monsters would find nothing but an empty cliffside when they arrived moments later, their hungry eyes scanning the horizon for any trace of the prey that had eluded them for so long. Jonas had found his peace and, at last, reunited with Sarah in the quiet depths of the sea.

As the night deepened, the city remained cloaked in silence, its secrets buried beneath the waves, where only the restless ocean bore witness to the tragic end of Jonas's journey.

BOOK TWO:

Story Of Deprivation

He had mapped out a routine to maintain a semblance of normalcy amidst the ruins. Mornings were for cautious exploration, searching for water, canned food, and any supplies that might have been overlooked. Afternoons he spent reinforcing his defenses, stacking debris and scavenged materials against windows and doors. Evenings were the hardest, as darkness descended and with it, the eerie cries and movements of the creatures outside grew louder.

Nights were when Adam found himself plagued the most by memories. He would sit by a cracked window, staring out into the gloom, replaying the scenes of chaos in his mind. The loss of his family was a wound that never seemed to heal, each recollection reopening it with brutal clarity. He had been powerless then, as he was now, against the relentless tide of despair that threatened to engulf him.

Amid this desolation, however, Adam found solace in small victories. The day he found a stash of batteries that still held charge, allowing him to power a radio and hear a faint, distant voice on the airwaves. Or the time he discovered a cache of medical supplies that kept him from succumbing to sickness. These moments sustained him, reminding him that despite the world crumbling around him, he could still endure.

But it was the loneliness that gnawed at him most relentlessly. He yearned for companionship, for someone to share the burden of survival. He often found himself talking aloud, imagining conversations with the ghosts of his past, seeking reassurance where none could be found.

As weeks turned into months, Adam's existence became a fragile balance between resilience and resignation. He had survived this long through sheer determination, but he knew he couldn't continue like this indefinitely. The city held too many painful memories, and the constant threat of the creatures outside wore down his defenses, both physical and emotional.

Yet, as Adam stood at the window one evening, gazing out at the darkened streets below, a new determination stirred within him. Perhaps there were other survivors out there, clinging to hope in their hidden sanctuaries. Perhaps, against all odds, he could find them, and together they could reclaim some semblance of the life that had been stolen from them.

With that thought, Adam turned away from the window, his mind racing with plans and possibilities. For the first time in a long while, a flicker of hope ignited in his heart, pushing back against the darkness that threatened to consume him. He knew the journey ahead would be perilous, fraught with unknown dangers and challenges, but he was no longer willing to merely survive.

Adam was ready to fight for a future, however uncertain it might be.

The next morning, Adam woke with a renewed sense of purpose. He carefully packed a bag with essentials: a few cans of food, a water bottle, a flashlight, and the map he had been sketching with locations of supplies and potential dangers marked. His plan was to venture beyond the familiar streets, to explore areas he had avoided due to the creatures' presence and the haunting memories they invoked.

Stepping out of his fortified sanctuary, Adam felt the weight of solitude press upon him once more. The city seemed to hold its breath around him, buildings leaning wearily against each other, streets cracked and overgrown. He moved silently, sticking to the shadows, hyper-aware of every sound - the distant shuffle of debris, the creak of metal, the occasional far-off growl that signaled the creatures' proximity.

As he navigated through the ruins, Adam encountered remnants of what life used to be: shattered storefronts with their goods long looted, abandoned vehicles choked with dust and rubble, and occasional graffiti marking desperate messages or warnings left by others who had passed through.

Hours passed as Adam moved deeper into uncharted territory. He found himself in neighborhoods where silence was more oppressive, the signs of human habitation more sparse. The sun climbed high in the sky, casting long shadows that seemed to reach out to him, whispering caution.

It was in one of these desolate neighborhoods that Adam stumbled upon a faint trail of footprints in the dust. Heart racing, he followed them cautiously, each step filled with anticipation and dread. The footprints led him to a building that appeared more intact than most - its windows, though cracked, were not boarded up, and a faded sign above the door hinted at a long-abandoned shop.

Adam approached cautiously, his senses on high alert. He pushed open the door slowly, wincing at the creak of rusted hinges. Inside, the air was stale and heavy with the scent of decay. His flashlight swept across shelves stripped bare, scattered debris, and signs of a hurried departure.

Just as he was about to turn away, a voice startled him from the shadows. "Who goes there?"

Adam spun around, flashlight beam darting across the dim interior. There, huddled in a corner, was a figure cloaked in shadows. A mix of relief and caution washed over him. "My name is Adam," he replied, voice steady despite the tremor in his limbs. "I'm just looking for survivors."

The figure hesitated for a moment, then stepped forward into the light. It was a woman, her face lined with weariness but her eyes bright with a flicker of hope. "I'm Sarah," she said, her voice hoarse from disuse. "I thought I was the only one left."

They stood there for a moment, sizing each other up, each searching the other's face for signs of trustworthiness. Then, slowly, Adam lowered his bag to the ground, a tentative smile tugging at his lips. "You're not alone anymore," he said softly.

Sarah's answering smile held a world of gratitude and relief. As they exchanged stories of survival and loss, plans began to form - a partnership forged in the crucible of their shattered world. Together, Adam and Sarah would face the challenges ahead, their shared determination a beacon against the encroaching darkness.

Outside, the city lay in ruins, its secrets and perils still waiting to be uncovered. But within the walls of the abandoned shop, Adam and Sarah found a flicker of hope, a promise of resilience in the face of despair. And as they looked out into the uncertain future, they knew that as long as they had each other, they would not just survive - they would strive to reclaim what had been lost, one step at a time.

Weeks turned into months as Adam and Sarah navigated the treacherous urban landscape together. They fortified their sanctuary, pooled their resources, and devised strategies to evade the creatures that roamed the streets. Their bond grew stronger with each passing day, a fragile yet resilient thread woven through the tapestry of their survival.

But as time wore on, ominous signs began to manifest. The creatures seemed to grow more aggressive, their nocturnal prowls encroaching closer to the boundaries of Adam and Sarah's refuge. Supplies dwindled despite their careful rationing, and their makeshift defenses showed signs of wear and vulnerability.

One fateful night, as Adam stood watch by a cracked window, scanning the shadows for any movement, he spotted something that froze his blood. In the distance, beyond the rubble-strewn streets, he saw a faint glimmer of light - not the cold, haunting glow of the creatures' eyes, but something different, something unmistakably human.

He nudged Sarah awake, his voice barely a whisper. "Sarah, look," he breathed, pointing towards the distant glow. She followed his gaze, her eyes widening in disbelief and apprehension. Together, they watched as the light flickered, distant but unmistakably real, a beacon of hope amidst the darkness.

"We're not alone," Sarah murmured, her voice tinged with equal parts relief and fear.

Adam nodded grimly. "We need to investigate. It could be survivors like us."

The decision weighed heavily on them both. They knew the risks of leaving their sanctuary, of exposing themselves to the dangers that lurked outside. Yet the allure of human contact, of companionship and shared struggle, pulled at their hearts like a magnetic force.

The next morning, armed with renewed determination and a sense of cautious optimism, Adam and Sarah prepared to venture towards the distant light. They left behind a note, a message of hope for anyone who might stumble upon their sanctuary, before setting out into the unknown once more.

As they navigated through the crumbling remnants of the city, each step brought them closer to the source of the light. Their senses were heightened, every sound and movement scrutinized for signs of danger or salvation. The journey was fraught with tension, their nerves stretched taut like bowstrings.

Finally, they reached the outskirts of a once-grand plaza, now reduced to a desolate wasteland of shattered statues and overgrown foliage. And there, amidst the ruins, they saw it - a flickering campfire, surrounded by figures huddled together in the fading twilight.

Relief washed over Adam and Sarah as they approached cautiously, heartbeats echoing in their ears. But as they drew nearer, a chill ran down Adam's spine. The figures around the campfire turned towards them slowly, revealing faces gaunt with hunger and eyes that gleamed with a mix of desperation and suspicion.

One figure stepped forward, a grim smile twisting their lips. "Welcome," they said, voice hollow and weary. "You've found us."

Adam exchanged a glance with Sarah, uncertainty clouding their expressions. They had found survivors, yes, but at what cost? As the campfire crackled and the wind whispered through the ruins, the realization dawned on them both - they had stepped into a new chapter of their struggle for survival.

BOOK THREE:

Story of War

Alone amidst the desolation, Sergeant Donovan surveyed the shattered remnants. The streets were littered with debris and the twisted remnants of the monstrous creatures that now ruled the city. They were relentless, their hunger insatiable, their forms distorted and horrifying.

Donovan had been separated from his unit longer than he cared to count. When the nightmare began, chaos had erupted - screams, gunfire, the guttural roars of the creatures. His comrades fell one by one, overwhelmed by the sheer numbers and ferocity of the enemy. Donovan himself had narrowly escaped, retreating deeper into the heart of the city as his radio crackled with cries for help and desperate pleas for reinforcements that would never come.

Now, he found himself holed up in an abandoned command post, the last remaining stronghold in this once-bustling sector. The walls were scarred with bullet holes, makeshift barricades hastily erected to fend off the relentless assaults. Donovan had scavenged what little ammunition and supplies remained, rationing them carefully as each day blurred into the next, a grim cycle of fighting and waiting.

Memories of fallen comrades haunted him, their faces etched in his mind - friends who had fought bravely, who had stood by his side until the bitter end. Their sacrifices weighed heavily on his shoulders, a burden he carried with grim determination.

As the sun dipped below the horizon, casting long shadows across the desolate streets, Donovan prepared himself for another night of relentless combat. The creatures would come, as they always did, drawn by the scent of blood and fear. He checked his weapon, the familiar weight a comfort in this sea of uncertainty. The radio crackled to life sporadically, distant voices pleading for any sign of hope, any glimmer of salvation.

Hours passed in tense silence broken only by sporadic bursts of gunfire and the agonized cries of the creatures as they fell to Donovan's relentless defense. Each wave seemed fiercer than the last, their numbers seemingly endless. But Donovan fought on, driven by a stubborn will to protect what little remained of humanity in this forsaken city.

Just as exhaustion threatened to overwhelm him, a faint sound caught his attention - a distant roar, deeper and more primal than any he had heard before. Donovan's heart sank as he realized what it meant - a new breed of creature, larger and more dangerous than anything they had faced thus far.

The ground trembled beneath his feet as the creature approached, its footsteps shaking the very foundation of the command post. Donovan braced himself, his mind racing with desperate calculations. He knew he couldn't hold them off forever, not against this new threat. His ammunition was running low, his defenses weakening with each passing moment.

But then, amidst the chaos and despair, a glimmer of hope - the distant sound of helicopters approaching, their rotors slicing through the night air. Reinforcements, at long last. Donovan's heart surged with renewed determination as he fought off the final onslaught of creatures, buying precious moments for the helicopters to arrive.

As the first helicopter touched down amidst the ruins, Donovan sprinted towards it, adrenaline coursing through his veins. He was greeted by fellow soldiers, faces weary but determined, their presence a lifeline in this sea of darkness.

"We've got survivors," Donovan gasped between breaths, adrenaline and relief mixing in his voice. "We need to evacuate them, now."

The soldiers nodded grimly, their expressions mirroring Donovan's urgency. Together, they formed a perimeter around the remaining civilians, guiding them toward the waiting helicopters as the creatures' howls grew more desperate and frenzied.

But as Donovan glanced back at the city skyline, a foreboding sense of unease settled over him. The battle was far from over. The creatures may have been pushed back for now, but they were relentless in their pursuit. As the last helicopter lifted off into the night sky, carrying with it the survivors and the soldiers who had fought so bravely, Donovan knew that the war for humanity's survival had only just begun.

As the city burned below, consumed by the chaos and despair, Donovan, soldier, and survivor, stared out into the darkness, steeling himself.

The helicopter's rotors thudded steadily, but in the back of his mind, Donovan could hear the relentless howls of the creatures, their monstrous forms still etched in his vision.

"Touchdown in ten minutes," the pilot's voice crackled over the intercom. Donovan checked his weapon one last time, his fingers brushing over the scarce ammunition he had left. Reinforcements had arrived, but the tide of the battle was turning into a flood of monstrous wrath.

The helicopter descended into the heart of a makeshift military base hastily erected on the outskirts of the city. Soldiers scurried about, fortifying defenses and tending to the wounded. Adam's boots hit the ground, and he was immediately engulfed in a flurry of activity. His comrades, their faces pale and drawn, nodded at him with respect.

"Sergeant Donovan," a young lieutenant called out, sprinting towards him. "We've been briefed on your situation. The monsters are evolving, becoming stronger and more aggressive. Our intel suggests a larger, more coordinated attack is imminent."

Donovan nodded grimly. "What's our plan, Lieutenant?"

The lieutenant pointed towards a massive map spread across a table. "We're setting up a final line of defense here, at the city's central power grid. If we can hold them off and keep the grid running, we might have a chance at coordinating a larger evacuation and counter-attack. But the creatures have been spotted in unprecedented numbers, and our scouts report a new type, something bigger and smarter."

As the plan unfolded, Donovan felt a flicker of hope but knew the reality: they were vastly outnumbered and under-prepared. The next wave of creatures would be unlike anything they had faced before.

Hours later, Donovan found himself entrenched behind a barricade, the night air filled with tension. The power grid loomed behind them, its humming an eerie backdrop to the silence. He looked around at the soldiers beside him, their faces a mix of determination and fear.

The first sign of the oncoming assault was a deep, rumbling growl that seemed to shake the earth itself. Shadows moved in the distance, grotesque and distorted shapes emerging from the darkness. The creatures charged, their eyes glowing with malevolent hunger.

"Hold the line!" Donovan shouted, his voice cutting through the noise. The soldiers opened fire, bullets tearing into the front ranks of the monstrosities. The creatures fell, but more surged forward, their bodies twisting and reforming even as they were struck down.

Suddenly, a deafening roar pierced the night, and a new breed of creature emerged. It was massive, its hulking form covered in thick, armored hide. It moved with terrifying speed, plowing through the defenses with ease. Bullets seemed to bounce off its skin, and its claws slashed through the air, ripping through metal and flesh alike.

"Focus fire on the big one!" Donovan ordered, aiming his rifle at the beast's head. He squeezed the trigger, but the creature barely flinched, its eyes burning with a sinister intelligence.

Donovan's heart pounded as he watched the beast shrug off their most potent attacks. The soldiers around him were fighting valiantly, but their efforts were becoming increasingly futile against the relentless onslaught.

Explosions and gunfire filled the air, but the monstrous tide was unstoppable. The smaller creatures swarmed the barricades, their numbers overwhelming the defenders. One by one, Donovan's comrades fell, their cries of pain and despair lost in the cacophony of battle.

Donovan's mind raced as he saw the situation deteriorate. He glanced towards the power grid, their last hope. The structure still stood, but the defenses around it were crumbling fast. He had to make a choice: continue the hopeless fight or try to buy more time for an evacuation.

"Fall back to the grid!" he yelled, his voice hoarse. "We need to hold them off as long as we can!"

The remaining soldiers obeyed, retreating towards the power grid in a desperate bid to regroup. Donovan's legs burned as he ran, his breath coming in ragged gasps. He could hear the creatures gaining ground, their guttural roars echoing in his ears.

They reached the power grid and quickly set up a final line of defense. The few remaining soldiers formed a tight perimeter, their faces grim and determined. Donovan took a moment to catch his breath, his eyes scanning the horizon for any sign of reinforcements.

But there were none. The radio was dead, and the sky remained dark. The realization hit him like a punch to the gut: they were truly alone.

"Hold them off as long as you can!" Donovan shouted, rallying his troops. "We need to give the civilians more time to escape!"

The creatures came in waves, their numbers seemingly endless. The soldiers fought with everything they had, but it was a losing battle. The new breed of monster tore through their defenses with terrifying ease, its claws slicing through steel and flesh alike.

Donovan fired his last round and dropped his empty rifle, grabbing a nearby soldier's discarded weapon. His body ached, and blood trickled down his face from a cut he couldn't remember receiving. But he kept fighting, driven by sheer willpower.

Minutes felt like hours as they held the line, but the inevitable was approaching. The creatures breached the perimeter, and chaos erupted. Donovan fought hand-to-hand, using anything he could as a weapon. He watched his comrades fall one by one, their sacrifices buying precious seconds.

Amid the carnage, Donovan found himself face-to-face with the massive creature. Its eyes glowed with malevolent intelligence, and a twisted grin spread across its face as it lunged at him. Donovan barely managed to dodge its attack, the creature's claws grazing his side.

Pain seared through him, but he refused to give in. He grabbed a nearby grenade and pulled the pin, charging at the beast with a primal roar. The creature swiped at him again, but this time, Donovan was ready. He ducked under its attack and slammed the grenade into its gaping maw.

The explosion rocked the battlefield, and the creature let out an ear-piercing screech. It staggered, its body convulsing as flames consumed it. But even as it fell, more creatures surged forward, their hunger insatiable.

Donovan collapsed to his knees, exhaustion and blood loss taking their toll. He looked around, seeing the few remaining soldiers being overwhelmed. The power grid was still intact, but it wouldn't be for long.

As darkness closed in, Adam's thoughts turned to his fallen comrades, their faces flashing before his eyes. They had fought bravely, but it hadn't been enough. The city, the world, was lost.

BOOK FOUR:

The Experiment

Simon Hartman stood at the edge of the chaos, his heart heavy with guilt and dread. From his vantage point in the underground bunker, he watched through the monitors as the last bastion of human resistance crumbled under the onslaught of the very creatures he had helped create. He had never imagined it would come to this—the project meant to advance humanity had turned into its greatest nightmare.

The bunker was a sterile environment, filled with the hum of computers and the flicker of screens displaying the horror above. Simon, one of the few surviving scientists, had locked himself away with the hope of finding a solution. The lab was a maze of equipment, papers scattered everywhere, and the remnants of failed experiments.

He rubbed his tired eyes, his mind replaying the events that had led to this apocalypse. The project, codenamed Genesis, was supposed to harness the power of genetic manipulation to create super-soldiers, beings capable of withstanding any threat. But something had gone horribly wrong. The creatures had evolved beyond control, their intelligence and savagery surpassing all predictions.

A sudden noise snapped Simon out of his reverie. The door to the lab creaked open, and a figure stumbled in, covered in blood and dirt. It was Dr. Elena Vasquez, his colleague and one of the few remaining members of their team.

"Simon," she gasped, her voice trembling. "They're everywhere. We need to leave. Now."

Simon shook his head, his face pale. "Leave? Where can we go? The whole city is overrun. There's no escape."

Elena grabbed his arm, her grip firm despite her exhaustion. "We can't just stay here and wait to die. There must be something we can do. Something we haven't tried."

Simon glanced at the screens again, the images of carnage fueling his determination. "There is one thing. But it's risky, and it might already be too late."

Elena's eyes widened. "What is it?"

Simon took a deep breath. "Project Lazarus. It's an experimental protocol we developed in case Genesis went wrong. It's a last-ditch effort to regain control over the creatures by using a neural override. It could potentially shut them down, but it requires direct access to the central node at the power grid."

Elena nodded, her expression resolute. "Then we have to try. It's our only chance."

They quickly gathered what they needed: a portable terminal, a series of neural transmitters, and a small arsenal of weapons. The bunker had a hidden exit that led to the outskirts of the city, a path they had hoped never to use. As they made their way through the tunnels, the sounds of destruction grew louder.

Emerging into the night, Simon and Elena moved cautiously, sticking to the shadows. The city was a warzone, fires burning unchecked, and the air thick with smoke. The power grid loomed in the distance, a beacon of hope and despair.

Their journey was fraught with danger. They encountered small groups of creatures, managing to evade some and fight off others. Each encounter took a toll, but they pressed on, driven by the knowledge that this was their last chance.

Finally, they reached the perimeter of the power grid. The defenses had fallen, and the area was swarming with creatures. Simon and Elena exchanged a determined glance, knowing what they had to do.

"Cover me while I set up the terminal," Simon instructed, his hands shaking as he began to work.

Elena took position, her weapon ready. The creatures sensed their presence, turning their attention towards the intruders. Bullets flew, and monstrous roars filled the air as Elena fought to keep them at bay.

Simon connected the terminal to the mainframe, his fingers flying over the keyboard. "Almost there," he muttered, sweat dripping down his face. The creatures were closing in, their numbers overwhelming.

"Simon, hurry!" Elena shouted, her voice strained as she fired her last rounds.

A deafening roar echoed through the power grid, and Simon's heart sank. The massive creature, the new breed, appeared, its eyes fixed on them with a deadly intelligence. Time was running out.

With a final keystroke, Simon activated Project Lazarus. The terminal beeped, and a signal pulsed through the grid. The creatures froze, their movements jerky and uncoordinated. For a moment, it seemed like the plan might work.

But then, the massive creature roared again, and the signal faltered. The neural override was failing, the creatures adapting faster than anticipated. Desperation clawed at Simon as he tried to reinforce the signal, but it was too late.

The creatures surged forward, their rage renewed. Elena screamed as they overwhelmed her, and Simon watched in horror as his friend and colleague was torn apart.

In a final act of defiance, Simon grabbed a transmitter and jammed it into his own neck. Pain exploded in his head as he tried to link directly to the neural network, hoping to amplify the signal with his own brain. The world around him blurred, and he felt the creatures' minds pressing against his.

For a brief, agonizing moment, Simon managed to push back. The creatures hesitated, their advance slowing. But the strain was too much. His vision darkened, and he collapsed, the transmitter sparking and failing.

As consciousness slipped away, Simon's mind wandered back to the beginning of the nightmare.

The Genesis project had started with the best intentions. In a world increasingly fraught with conflict and danger, the goal was to create super-soldiers who could protect humanity. Using a combination of genetic manipulation and advanced neural enhancements, the team sought to push the boundaries of human potential. They aimed to create beings who could heal rapidly, possess extraordinary strength and speed, and have heightened senses. These beings were to be humanity's ultimate protectors.

But the experiments had gone awry. Early trials had shown promise, but there were unexpected side effects. The subjects, dubbed "Shadow People" due to their ability to move with preternatural stealth and their dark, almost translucent skin, began to exhibit aggressive behavior. Their intelligence increased exponentially, but so did their savagery.

As the Shadow People evolved, they developed a hive-mind mentality, communicating through a form of telepathy. This made them more coordinated and deadly. Attempts to contain them failed spectacularly. Once they breached containment, the Shadow People quickly overran the facility, and the contagion spread to the city.

In desperation, the scientists developed Project Lazarus, a neural override meant to shut down the Shadow People's hive mind. But it had always been a long shot, a final, desperate gamble.

As the creatures closed in, Simon's final thoughts were of regret and determination. They had created monsters, but they had also tried to undo their mistake. As darkness consumed him, he hoped that someone, somewhere, would learn from their errors and find a way to stop the Shadow People once and for all.

The creatures swarmed over his lifeless body, their victory complete. The city lay in ruins, the last remnants of human resistance extinguished.

www.ingramcontent.com/pod-product-compliance
Lightning Source LLC
Chambersburg PA
CBHW061635050726
47502CB00012B/2255